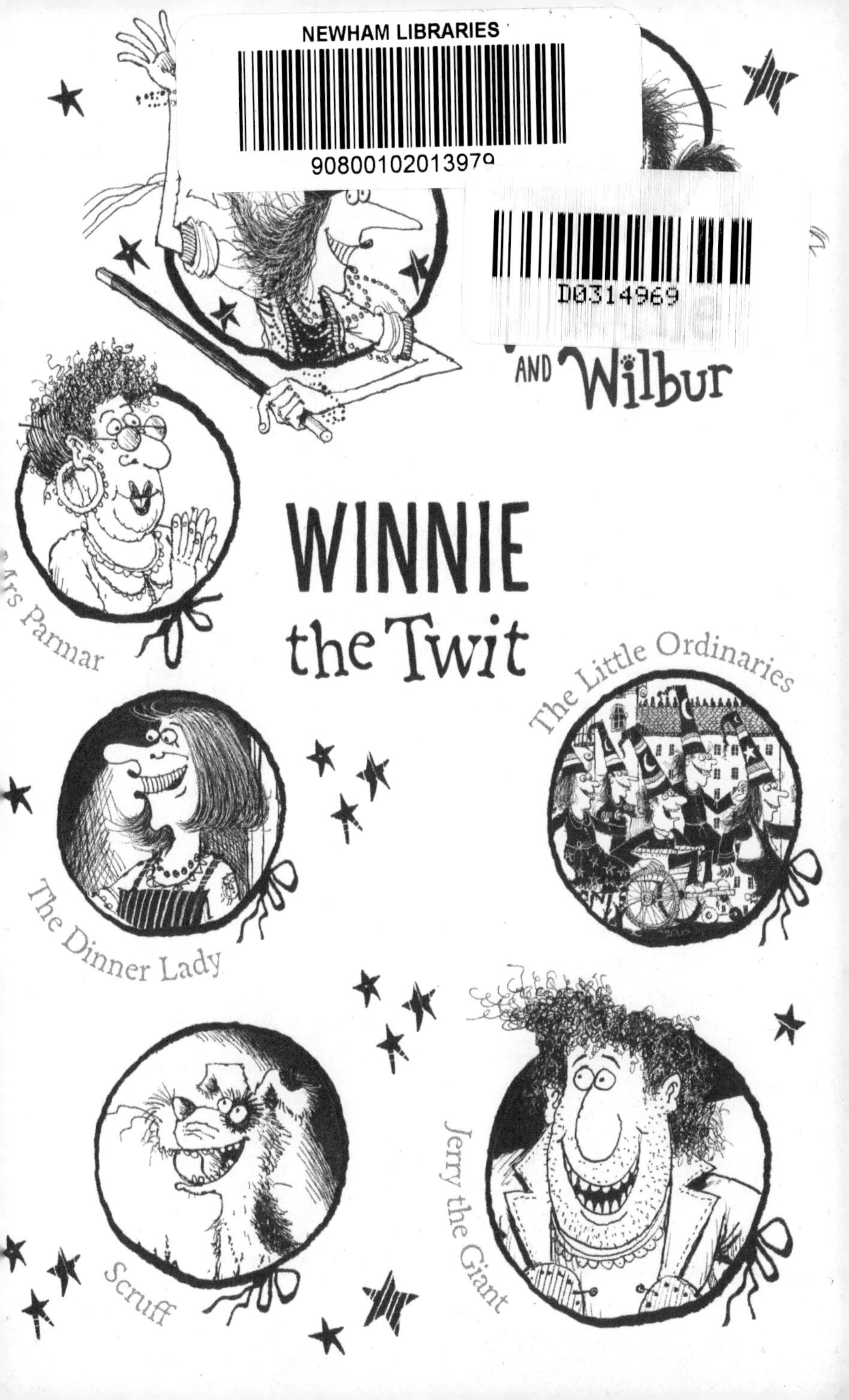

AND Wilbur
WINNIE
the Twit
Mrs Parmar
The Little Ordinaries
The Dinner Lady
Scruff
Jerry the Giant

For Jac – K.P.
For Susie Goodhart, with love – xx

OXFORD
UNIVERSITY PRESS

Great Clarendon Street, Oxford OX2 6DP

Oxford University Press is a department of the University of Oxford. It furthers the University's objective of excellence in research, scholarship, and education by publishing worldwide. Oxford is a registered trade mark of Oxford University Press in the UK and in certain other countries

First published in 2009
This edition first published in 2016

British Library Cataloguing in Publication Data
Data available

ISBN: 978-0-19-274835-5 (paperback)

2 4 6 8 10 9 7 5 3 1

Printed in Great Britain

Paper used in the production of this book is a natural, recyclable product made from wood grown in sustainable forests. The manufacturing process conforms to the environmental regulations of the country of origin.

LAURA OWEN & KORKY PAUL

Winnie AND Wilbur

WINNIE the Twit

OXFORD
UNIVERSITY PRESS

CONTENTS

WINNIE'S Perfect Pet

7

WINNIE Fixes It

29

Disgusting DINNERS

WINNIE the Twit

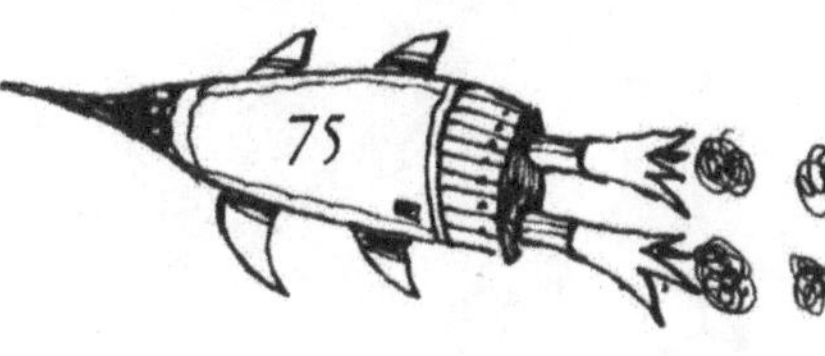

WINNIE'S
Perfect Pet

Wilbur was lying in the sun on the front doorstep, slumped in the sunshine, when Winnie came rushing over.

'Wilbur!' she said. 'Oh, Wilbur, there's a **huge** man as big as a ginormous giraffe moved in next door! And he's as rude as a bee's fluffy bottom! He called me a scruff!'

Wilbur opened one eye. He looked at Winnie, then he closed the eye again.

'Play with me, Wilbur,' said Winnie.

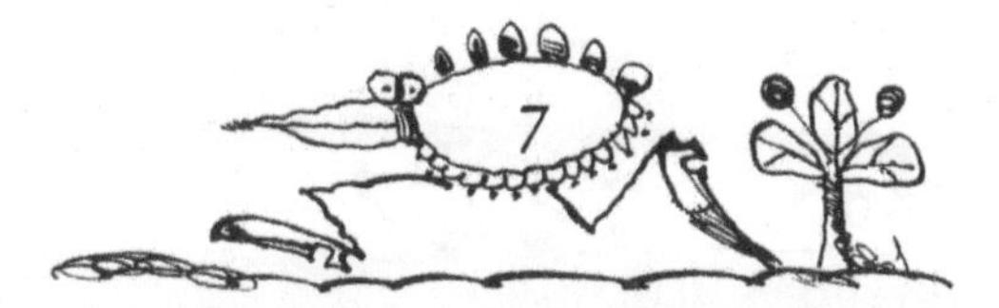

'Take my mind off that rude man. That's what a good pet would do.'

Wilbur yawned. He got up slowly, arched his back high, stretched his legs long, then sagged back into snoozing.

'You're as lazy as a hot lizard full of lunch!' said Winnie. 'Come on, let's play tennis, Wilbur!'

Winnie rushed indoors. She crashed through the kitchen. She bumped through the battery. She wriggled through the wormery. She skipped through the spidery. Then she came to the hall where she tugged open the door under the stairs, and out fell . . . everything!

'There it is!'

Winnie pounced. First, she tugged at something grey and tatty. Then she pulled out something that looked like a big holey spoon, and something else that looked like a mouldy old orange. She nipped into the loo . . . and came out looking like . . . um . . . this!

Winnie skipped, wriggled, bumped, and crashed back outside.

'What d'you think, Wilbur?'

Wilbur just put his paws over his face.

Winnie bounced the ball all around Wilbur. **Bounce, bounce.** 'Come on,' she said. 'Time to play!'

Wilbur didn't move.

'You're no fun,' said Winnie. 'I'll play with magic, if you won't play.'

Winnie pointed her wand at the racket and ball. 'Abracadabra, abracadabra, abracadabra!' she shouted.

In an instant there were three tennis rackets and three more balls, all in the air. The rackets were hitting balls at Winnie.

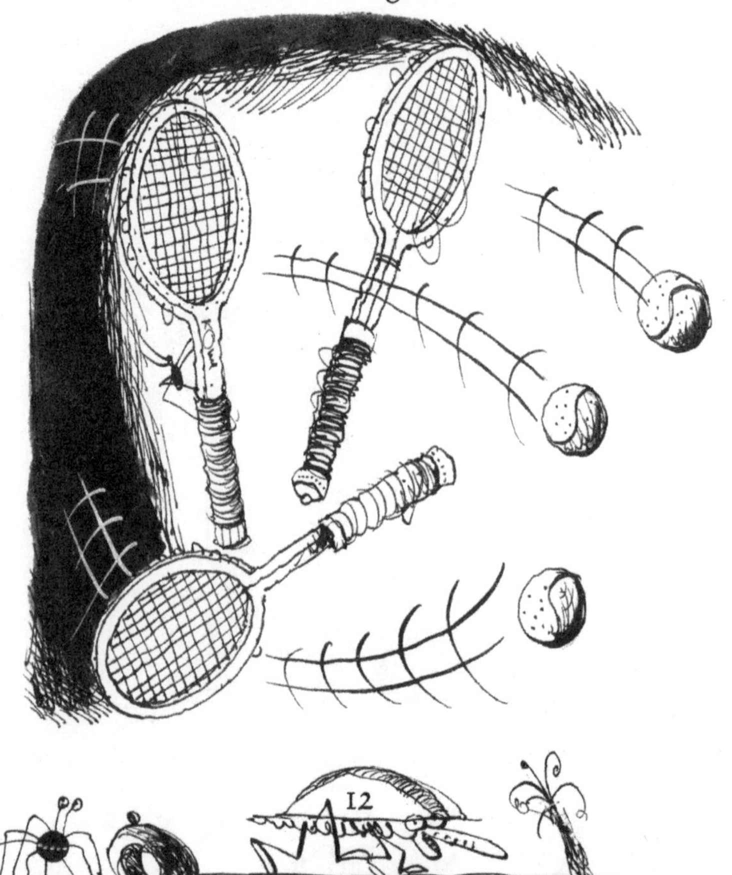

Winnie waved her own racket, up 'Hup!', down **'Ooph!'**, around **'Aah!'**, but she missed every ball.

'Ow! Ouch! Get off! Stop!' she shouted. 'Gnats' knickers!' she said. 'Nobody's nice to me today, not even my wand!'

Winnie picked up her wand and she threw it far into the undergrowth but, a moment later, the wand was back . . . in the mouth of a dog.

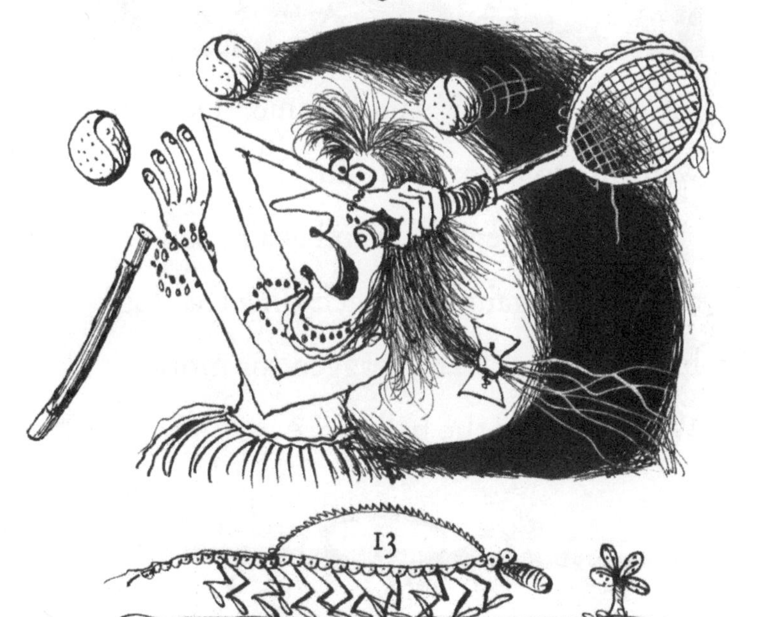

The dog came bounding up to Winnie. It dropped the wand at Winnie's feet, then grinned up at her and wagged its tail.

'Who are you?' said Winnie. 'Do you want me to throw it again?'

Winnie threw the wand again, and again, and again. And each time the dog brought it back and wagged for more. Winnie threw the ball too.

'Fetch!'

Back came the dog with the ball.

'Clever boy! Did you see that, Wilbur? Isn't he a clever dog?'

'Mreow,' said Wilbur.

'Don't you like him?' said Winnie. 'I do. I like him ever so much. Let's all have lunch together.'

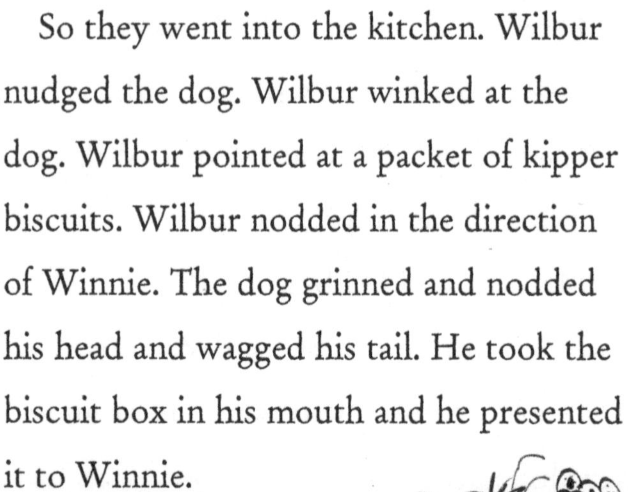

So they went into the kitchen. Wilbur nudged the dog. Wilbur winked at the dog. Wilbur pointed at a packet of kipper biscuits. Wilbur nodded in the direction of Winnie. The dog grinned and nodded his head and wagged his tail. He took the biscuit box in his mouth and he presented it to Winnie.

‘For me?’ said Winnie, not really looking. ‘Oh, isn’t he a good dog, Wilbur?’ Winnie dipped a hand into the box, then popped a biscuit into her mouth.

‘Euch! Pah!’ spat Winnie. ‘Yuck! Horrible, horrible! Kipper biscuits, I hate ’em!’ She danced around, making faces and waggling her tongue.

The dog hid under the table.

Wilbur puffed out his chest and grinned. Then he prepared a tray with Winnie's really favourite lunch snacks. Crispy worms. A nettle sandwich. A cup of slug smoothie.

'Yummy!' said Winnie. 'You're the *really* clever boy, Wilbur. You know just what I like!'

But the dog stuck out a leg and . . .

Trip! went Wilbur. **Crash!** went the tray.

Splat! went the smoothie, while crispy worms rained down on Winnie.

'Oh, Wilbur, you're as clumsy as a centipede on skates!' shouted Winnie.

Wilbur and the dog were busy sticking tongues out at each other. But, 'I've just had a brillaramaroodle idea!' said Winnie, perking up. 'Can you two guess what it is?'

The dog and Wilbur both shook their heads. 'It's obvious!' said Winnie. 'Cats are clever and dogs are obedient. I want a pet that's both of those things, so what I need is a *cog*!'

'Yowl!' went the dog.

'Mrrreow!' went Wilbur.

They both raced for the door, but Winnie was already stirring with her wand. 'Abracadabra!'

Magic whirled and swirled, and in an instant there was . . . a cog.

'Perfect,' said Winnie.

But the cog was not perfect. It bounded up the curtains and chewed them to bits.

'MEEEEOW-WOOF!' Chew-chew, munch.

Winnie reached out a hand. 'Good cog,' she said.

But the cog hissed at her. Then it lifted its leg and weed on her foot.

'Euch! Bad cog!' said Winnie.

The cog jumped onto the sink, then out of the window into the garden. It began to dig.

'Come back!' shouted Winnie.

The cog took no notice. It dug a big muddy hole. It rolled in the mud. Then it sat and lifted a leg and licked the mud off it. It sniffed Winnie's bottom, then it jumped up at Winnie with muddy paws and scratchy claws.

'Get down!' said Winnie. 'Sit! Naughty boy! Wilbur, save me!'

But of course Wilbur wasn't there. Oh, dear, thought Winnie. This cog isn't the best bits of a dog mixed with the best bits of a cat after all. It's the worst of both of them joined together!

'Where's my wand? I want my Wilbur back.'

Winnie saw the wand on the ground. The cog saw it too, and it began to run towards the wand, its teeth snip-snapping.

'It's *my* wand!' shouted Winnie as she leapt into a magnificent dive, up and over and down, to grab the wand, and waved it—'Abracadabra!'—just as the cog's teeth were about to snap it in two.

Then there was Wilbur, looking shocked but pleased. And there was the dog, running away down the drive.

'Scruff!' boomed a big voice.

Winnie put her hands on her hips. 'It's that rude man again,' she said. 'He's as rude as ten frogs' bottoms, he is!'

But the dog was jumping around the man, wagging its tail and woofing.

'Scruffy, my dear old Scruff!' laughed the man.

Then Winnie smiled. 'Know what, Wilbur?' she said. 'It's the dog that's a Scruff, not me! There's nothing wrong with me after all. And nothing wrong with you either, come to that. Give us a kiss, Wilbur!'

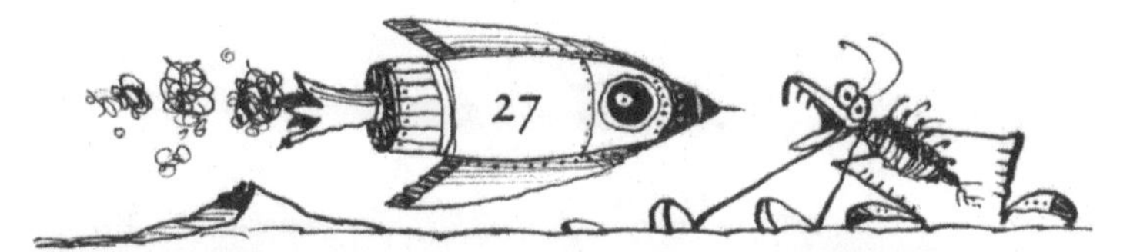

Wands
WITCH ONE
WITCH ONE

WINNIE
Fixes It

'See this, Wilbur?' asked Winnie. She was waving *Witch One?* magazine under his nose. 'I want one of those conservatory things.'

Wilbur did a squint.

'What do I want it for?' said Winnie. 'For growing plants in, that's what. Just think, Wilbur, we could have our own jungle with creepers and vines. We could keep exotic insects in it!' Winnie licked

her lips. 'Oo, it makes me hungry just thinking about it! Right,' said Winnie. 'Stand back!' She pointed her wand at the picture.

In an instant, there stood a beautiful shiny glass conservatory. But, 'Oh, soggy babies' bottoms,' said Winnie.

The conservatory was perfect in every way . . . except for its size. It was the same size as the picture. 'I'll use it for keeping my toenail clippings in,' said Winnie, putting it on the table. 'Let's try again. Get it BIG this time, wand!' Winnie whacked the wand hard on the page.

'Abracadabra!'

Conser
70

Instantly Winnie and Wilbur were fighting something huge that flapped down on them from above.

'I can't see!' said Winnie. 'The sky has fallen! Where are you, Wilbur?'

Wilbur fought and spat and clawed and scratched and bit . . . and escaped from the giant magazine page. He hauled Winnie out from under it.

'Oh, nits' knickers!' said Winnie. 'Magic isn't going to work for this.'

Wilbur began to build a tower with bits of earwigs' earwax fudge.

'That's it, Wilbur!' said Winnie. 'Clever boy! We'll get a proper builder in to build us a conservatory, just like normal people do. Do we know a builder?'

Wilbur did.

'What?' said Winnie. 'That great big man from next door? Are you sure?'

Wilbur was right. There was a new sign up. 'Build Your Dreams with Jerry the Builder.'

'He's already done some work on his own house,' said Winnie. 'Look!'

Jerry had had to lift the roof and extend the doors of his house because Jerry was a giant.

'A big chap like that should be able to build things almost as fast as magic,' said Winnie. 'Shall we ask him if he's free?'

'People from the village, they sees my sign and they knocks on the door,' said Jerry, scratching his head. 'But they always runs away when I opens it. So I'm vacant at the moment, missus.'

So Jerry came with his dog and his bag of tools and his radio, and he set to work. But a big chap like Jerry didn't fit into Winnie's house very comfortably.

BEND, BUMP!

'Ouch!'

CRASH, BANG!

'Oooch!'

'Better build from the outside,' said Winnie.

But, 'Got to make a hole for where the conservatory will join the house,' said Jerry. 'Stand back, missus!' Jerry swung back a huge great mallet, then—**THUNK!**—he hit the wall. **CRASH!** Bricks tumbled, tiles tumbled, windows tumbled.

'Oh, no!' said Winnie.

A whole turret tumbled.

'Whoops!' said Jerry. 'Sorry, missus!'

Winnie's house was opened up like a doll's house. You could see all her bits and pieces, and Wilbur's too.

'That's not safe to go into now,' said Jerry. 'Not till I've put some beaming support whatnots in.' Jerry looked at his fob watch. 'It's time for me to finish for the day now. I'll see you tomorrow, missus.'

'Hang on a blooming mini-minute!' said Winnie, but Jerry had picked up his bag and was on his way.

'Well,' said Winnie, hands on hips. 'We'll just have to sleep in the garden like snails tonight.'

Winnie and Wilbur put a sleeping bag on the lawn.

'Eeek!' wailed Winnie. 'This grass is wet! We need a floor, Wilbur.'

So Winnie and Wilbur went to Jerry's building yard. They dragged back some planks, laid them down, and fixed them together. They put the sleeping bag onto their new floor.

'That's better,' said Winnie, snuggling into the bag.

'Yip yip!' came a noise from the woods.

'Snarl!'

'Hisss!'

'Howl!'

'Yip yip yip!'

Winnie sat up, with her hair on end. 'What the heck was that? Wilbur?'

Wilbur had buried himself deep in the sleeping bag.

'This is no blooming good,' said Winnie. 'We need some walls to keep us safe!'

So Winnie and Wilbur went back to Jerry's yard where they found some old windows. They fixed them up to make a wall.

'That's better!' said Winnie, snuggling down in the bag. 'Look at those stars, Wilbur! They're as beautiful as dandruff on velvet.'

Wilbur yawned. *Snore-purr.*

'We should sleep out here more often, Wilbur,' said Winnie.

Splat!

'What . . .?' began Winnie.

Split-splot!

'Mrrow!' Wilbur woke with a start. He'd suddenly turned into a black and white cat.

'He hee, look at you!' laughed Winnie. 'You look like a cow! Or a magpie!'

But then Winnie looked at herself. 'Oooo, yucky-horrible owls! We need a roof, that's what we need, Wilbur!'

So Winnie and Wilbur collected all the bits of broken glass that had fallen when Jerry made his hole.

'We just need some sticky-icky spider spit glue.' Winnie waved her wand over the broken glass. '*Abracadabra!*'

And instantly the bits of glass were joined together into a crazy kind of glass roof.

'That's fixed it!' said Winnie, snuggling down into the sleeping bag. Then she squinted. 'What the fish-toed heck is that?'

It was the sun, just beginning to come up.

'Oh, blooming blasted heck!' said Winnie, reaching for her wand again.

'*Abracadabra!*'

Instantly there were plants in pots, sheltering Winnie and Wilbur from the light.

Winnie and Wilbur slept at last, until . . . **THUMP THUMP** . . . footsteps woke them.

'Mornin', missus,' said Jerry, knocking on the glass. 'Gor, you've gone and built your own conservatory!'

'Have I?' said Winnie. 'But what a blooming mess! Where's my wand? **Abracadabra!**'

And instantly Winnie's conservatory smartened up and fixed itself to the house. Jerry scratched his head.

'Now I'm vacant again, with nuffink to do. Bovver.'

'Come and have a bite of breakfast with us,' said Winnie. 'D'you like poached toad on toast? With a cup of puddle tea? Wilbur's a really good cook.'

'But I can't fit in your kitchen, missus,' said Jerry.

'Then we'll just have to eat outside,' said Winnie. 'Hmmm. Y'know what this house needs? It needs one of those patio things.'

'I'll just get me mallet,' said Jerry.

Disgusting DINNERS

'I spy with my little eye-spy eye something beginning with "W",' said Winnie.

Wilbur pointed.

'Not "Winnie",' said Winnie. 'Not "witch" either!'

Wilbur sighed and pointed again.

'That's right!' said Winnie. 'It's my "wand"! Let's do another one. I spy with my little eye-spy eye something else beginning with "W".'

Wilbur yawned widely.

'Oh, you're blooming well right,' said Winnie. 'This is boring! I was going to do "wormery" and "watch" like usual. But then I'm stuck. If only we had a "wombat" or a "whippet" or . . . '

Wilbur shook his head.

'Don't look like that, Wilbur! I only know "W" things,' said Winnie. 'Do you think it's too late to go to school and learn more letters?'

They went to find out. The school in the village looked a bit like Winnie's house. But there were children running around in a playground and shouting.

'Look, Wilbur!' said Winnie. 'Lots of little ordinaries! Ring the doorbell.'

But the school secretary didn't want Winnie in her school. Mrs Parmar was big and scary, and so was her smile.

'This is a school for children, not for grown-up witches,' she said. 'Off you go!'

Winnie and Wilbur were just heading for the gate when a jolly lady waved out of the school's kitchen window.

'Excuse me,' said the lady. 'Is that cat busy? Only we've got mice in the store cupboard. Is that cat any good at catching mice?'

'Meeow!' said Wilbur proudly.

In a moment Wilbur was through the window and into the kitchen, chasing and pouncing and catching—**eek! squeak! tweak!**—three mice in one movement.

'The job's yours!' said the lady. 'You'll be paid in school dinners.'

'Ahem,' said Winnie. 'Any chance of a job for me as well, lady?'

'As a matter of fact, there is,' said the lady. 'Can you cook?'

'Can I cook? Are slugs slimy? Yes,' said Winnie. 'I'm ever so good at cooking.' She looked at the mice dangling in Wilbur's mouth. 'In fact I could use—'

But Wilbur slammed a paw over Winnie's mouth to stop her from finishing what she was going to say.

The lady gave Winnie the proper clothes and hat to wear for cooking.

'I've got to go now,' said the lady. 'But it's spaghetti bolognaise and ratatouille on the menu today. Good luck!' And off she went.

'Right,' said Winnie. 'Where do they keep the cauldrons? Let's get cooking. Ratatouille sounds yummy-scrummy. Look in the fridge, Wilbur, and bring out the rats.'

Wilbur looked in the fridge and in the larder. There were sacks of onions and boxes of aubergines and red and yellow peppers and courgettes, but no rats anywhere.

'Aha, I bet I know why,' said Winnie. 'They like things as fresh as possible for school dinners these days. You'll just have to catch the rats now, Wilbur. Quick as you can!'

Wilbur raced out of the door and into the sheds by the school field. *Leap, screech, wallop!* That was one rat caught. *Sneak, pounce, squeal!* That was another.

Meanwhile Winnie had remembered that the cook had said something about bolognaise.

'I do a lovely worm bolognaise,' said Winnie. 'I suppose those worms will have to be caught fresh as well.'

Off she went to the football pitch where she waved her wand.

'*Abracadabra!*'

Instantly, worms wriggled up from the ground and Winnie picked and pulled them and chucked them into a bucket.

Before long, Winnie and Wilbur were back in the kitchen, cooking as fast as they could.

Clang-clang!

'Dinner time already! Quick, Wilbur, put on a clean pinny and get ready to serve!'

Winnie heaved the cauldron onto the counter just as the children started to come through the door.

But somebody large was pushing to the front of the queue.

'Out of the way, children! Have some respect! Adults first!'

It was Mrs Parmar, pushing to the front. She thrust her tray towards Winnie. 'I'll have a large helping of that!' she said, pointing a fat finger at the cauldron.

Winnie ladled out wriggling worm bolognaise.

'This food is moving!' said Mrs Parmar.

'Just goes to show that it's really fresh,' said Winnie.

'In that case I'll have more of it!' said Mrs Parmar.

'Greedy pig!' said Winnie, but she ladled out more.

'And I'll have those novelty shape things too!' said Mrs Parmar, pointing at Wilbur's rats. 'I'll have three of those!'

Mrs Parmar sat down at a table and started to raise a forkful of worm bolognaise into her mouth. But a moment later she was shrieking.

'Euch!' *Spit!* 'Absolutely disgusting!'

Mrs Parmar was leaping around the place.

'You've poisoned me! Yeuch! What in the world have you fed me?'

'Ratatouille,' said Winnie. 'Made with lovely fresh rats. And bolognaise with freshly harvested worms. What's your problem?'

Mrs Parmar ran out of the hall.

But then Winnie noticed that it wasn't only Mrs Parmar who had a problem with the food. All the children were backing away from the serving hatch, hurrying to get out of the hall.

'Don't go, you little ordinaries!' called Winnie. 'Have your lunch!'

'But we don't want to eat worms and rats,' said a boy.

'Really?' said Winnie. 'How strange! Well, that's easily solved. What would you really like to eat, little boy?'

'Doughnuts!'

'Ice cream!'

'Easy-peasy lemon squeezy!' said Winnie. She took out her wand and she waved it over the food.

And instantly the rats and the worms were replaced by plates and plates of lovely party food.

'Yum!' shouted all the children, and they all ate lots. Winnie sat and ate and chatted with them. Wilbur showed off on the climbing equipment around the hall, while the children cheered him on.

Until Mrs Parmar came back in.

'Back to your classrooms, everyone!'

She waved a fat finger at Winnie.

'As for you!' said Mrs Parmar, her chins all wobbling. 'Clear away all this mess, and then go!'

'What about tomorrow?' asked Winnie. 'I thought I might do hot dogs.'

'Go!' said Mrs Parmar.

The clearing up was easy.

'Abracadabra!'

Instantly the kitchen was clean and tidy.

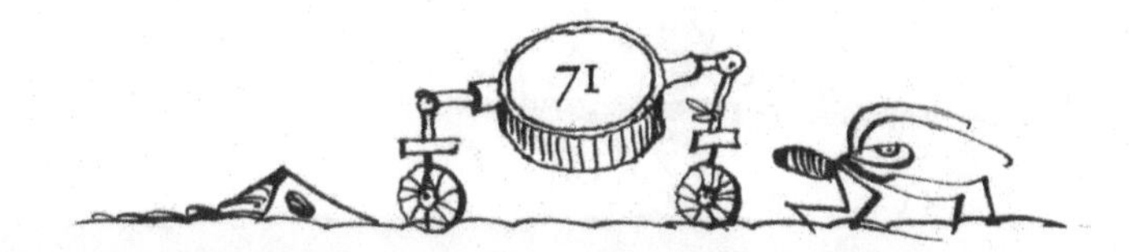

Then Winnie and Wilbur went home to their own dirty messy homely kitchen to cook their own tea.

'Ah, well,' sighed Winnie. 'At least there's one thing I learnt at school today.'

'Mrrow?' asked Wilbur.

'I've learnt a new letter,' said Winnie. 'Try this one, Wilbur. I spy with my little eye something beginning with "Q".'

Wilbur frowned. Wilbur looked around. Wilbur pointed.

'No!' said Winnie. 'Not a "quill". No, not a "quail" either. Nor the "Queen". D'you give up?'

Wilbur nodded.

'It's cucumber!'

'Mrrow!'

'What do you mean, cucumber doesn't begin with "Q"?' said Winnie. 'Listen to it . . . *cu*cumber!'

Wilbur sunk his head into his paws.

WINNIE
the Twit

'How many—' *slurp munch* '—have you got in your bucket, Wilbur?' asked Winnie.

They were picking dew-fresh caterpillars off pongberry trees.

Wilbur showed his bucket of wriggling, hairy, stripy caterpillars.

'Oo, well done, Wilbur! Yummy!' said Winnie. She opened her mouth wide, like a baby bird, and threw a caterpillar in. 'Mmn. I should stop eating them or there won't be

enough to make the jam. But they are so delicious, freshly picked!' Winnie poked a finger into her mouth to pick the bits of caterpillar stuck to her teeth. *Burp!* 'Isn't nature wonderful, Wilbur? It gives us everything we need.'

Wilbur sniffed a caterpillar, and sneezed. Tentatively, he nibbled a tiny bit of hairy caterpillar bottom.

'Meeeuch!' He spat it out!

'You'll like it when it's sweetened with sugar,' said Winnie.

Wilbur sighed and thought longingly of tinned tripe seasoned with fleas. He thought of snail slime lollies from the deep freeze. Wilbur sat down dreamily . . . straight onto a patch of stinging nettles.

'Meeeeooooww! Hissss!'

'You should pick them, not sit on them!' said Winnie. 'They make a lovely soup.'

'Ooo, look, a toad!' said Winnie, parting the long grass. 'There he goes!' Winnie dived like a goalkeeper . . . **weeeeooooww** . . . and caught the toad mid-hop.

'Ribbit!' said the toad.

'Got him!' shouted Winnie. 'We'll have Toad-in-the-Hole for lunch!'

'Ribbit!' went the toad, and it hopped on to Winnie's head and away.

'Quick, chase him!' shouted Winnie, but Wilbur raised an eyebrow.

'Oh, all right,' said Winnie. 'We'll just have Hole for lunch. Hole with nettle sauce. Then we'll make that jam.'

Most of the day was spent in the steamy kitchen, stirring cauldrons full of sticky caterpillar jam.

'Tip in more sugar, Wilbur!' said Winnie. She dipped in her wand and gave it a lick. 'Eeeek! Ouch! Too hot!'

She waved the wand to cool the jam, then licked again.

'Delicioso! Have a taste, Wilbur.'

Then suddenly Winnie went green. She clutched her tummy.

'Um,' she said. 'I think I've maybe had enough caterpillars for the moment.' She did a big burp. 'Actually, Wilbur, I think I'll just go outside for a bit of air.'

Winnie wandered out, and the beautiful red sun and pink sky behind upside-down broomstick trees soon made her forget her tummy.

'Absolutely blooming beeeeautiful!' sighed Winnie. 'Oo, did I hear something?'

'Twoo twit!'

'Snails in the sweet jar! Whatever was that?' Winnie's voice quivered. 'That sounded like an owl, but different somehow.'

'Twoo twit!'

'It must be a new kind of owl! Something rare, perhaps. Ooo, I must peek a look at it, and then I can tell Wilbur all about what he's missed!'

Winnie went tiptoeing into the wood.

'Twooo twit! Twoooo twit!' she called.

Winnie listened. There was no sound except the buzzing of evening midges. 'Has it flown away?' Winnie tried again. 'Twooo twit! Twooo twit! Twoooo twit!' And this time . . .

'Twoooo twit!' came a reply.

'Oh, oh!' went Winnie. She could hardly believe it! 'Twooo twit!' Winnie's eyes were darting here and there amongst the dark trees, looking for the owl. 'Twooo twit!' she called.

'Twooo twit!'

'Where are you, owly?' whispered Winnie, her hands clasped together. She waded through the tangle of plants, pushing them aside like a swimmer.

'Twooo twit!'

'Twooo twit!'

. . . And, **BUMP!** Winnie walked straight into something big and soft, and she bounced off it and landed on her bum.

'Knotted nanny goats! What the heck kind of an owl can it be?'

'Is you all right, missus?' asked a voice from above. It was Jerry, the giant from next door.

'Jerry?' said Winnie. 'What are you doing out here? Ssshh-up your big booming voice, you big lummox! There's a rare kind of an owl somewhere nearby, and I've almost caught it!'

'D'you mean that owl that calls backwards?' asked Jerry, offering a little finger to Winnie to help her pull herself back onto her feet.

'Ssshh! Have you seen it, then?' whispered Winnie. 'I've been calling it, and it's been answering me back!'

'Me too!' said Jerry.

'Ssshh! You too what?' asked Winnie.

'I've been calling "twooo twit", and that owl, it's been calling back to me, and . . . '

'Twooo twit?! You mean . . . ! Oh!' Winnie thumped Jerry hard. **Oooph!** 'That wasn't the owl! That was me calling back, you great steaming great noodle!'

'Well, you're a twit too, if you thought *I* was a bird!' laughed Jerry.

After a moment, Winnie's scowl melted into a smile. 'We could try being birds, if you like,' she said. 'D'you fancy flying, Jerry?' Before Jerry could say a thing, Winnie waved her wand. '*Abracadabra!*'

Next instant, Winnie and Jerry felt something hanging from their shoulders. They shrugged and found that the heavy somethings opened and closed behind them, pushing them forward.

'Eh? Wings, real wings!' said Jerry. He flip-flap-lurched up onto tiptoe, then up so that his big boots lifted off the ground. 'I'm flipping well flying, missus! I'm flittering and fluttering like a blooming butterfly!'

Jerry's wings were beautifully patterned, but butterflies don't usually weigh ten tonnes and kick and punch the air as they fly.

Winnie was up in the sky too. Her wings were black tatty bat wings, like old umbrellas. Up went Winnie.

'Weeee! I can loop the loop! I can fly upside down!'

Down below, Wilbur had come out of the house and was watching. He covered his eyes as Winnie looped. He wound a paw claw around his head to show that he thought she was as loopy as her loop. But Winnie was enjoying herself. 'Look at me! I'm going to land in a tree!'

But Jerry got to the tree first. **Crump!** He landed on a branch. It was Scruff who covered his eyes this time. There was a second of quiet, then **creeeeeak** . . . **CRASH!** Scruff covered his ears as the branch—and Jerry the butterfly—landed on the ground.

'Oh,' said Jerry. 'Ouch!' said Jerry, rubbing his bottom.

A very cross, very ordinary owl, rose up from the tree.

'Twit twoo!' he called.

'Twit yourself!' said Winnie, coming down to land. 'Ah, all that fresh air has given me an appetite. D'you know what I fancy?'

Wilbur shook his head.

'What?' said Jerry.

'I fancy anything at all as long as it doesn't taste of caterpillar!' said Winnie. 'Would you like some jars of caterpillar jam, Jerry?'

'Er . . .'

'On mushroom bread, and with a nice cup of puddle tea? I've got pots of the stuff going free if you'd like it. I think Wilbur and I are going to open a nice tin of tripe.'

'Purrrr!' went Wilbur, and he licked his lips.

Enjoy more magic moments with
Winnie AND Wilbur